Jutta Langreuter was born in Copenhagen, spent her childhood in Brussels, and now lives in Munich with her family. She worked with children for years as a professional psychologist. When her two sons were born, she started to write children's books and delights in creating them.

Stefanie Dahle was born in 1981 in the city of Schwerin in northern Germany. As a child she spent many happy hours in the company of picture books and in painting the walls of her room. She went on to study illustration in Hamburg, and today she creates her own beautiful and highly imaginative picture book worlds that invite one to linger and daydream. Since 2007 she has been working exclusively for the publishing house Arena Verlag.

Copyright © 2014 by Arena Verlag GmbH, Würzburg, Germany.
First published in Germany under the title *Ich bin so gerne mit dir zusammen*.
English translation copyright © 2017 by NorthSouth Books Inc.
Translated by David Henry Wilson.

First published in the United States, Great Britain, Canada, Australia, and New Zealand in 2017 by NorthSouth Books Inc., an imprint of NordSüd Verlag AG, CH-8005 Zürich, Switzerland.
Distributed in the United States by NorthSouth Books Inc., New York 10016.

Library of Congress Cataloging-in-Publication Data is available.
Printed in Latvia by Livonia Print, Riga, October 2016.
ISBN: 978-0-7358-4279-3
1 3 5 7 9 • 10 8 6 4 2

www.northsouth.com

MIX
Papier aus verantwor-
tungsvollen Quellen
FSC® C002795

Jutta Langreuter • Stefanie Dahle

So Happy Together!

North
South

"I'm going to the market," said Mommy Bunny. "I'll be back soon!"

"Ugh!" said Brayden Bunny, sitting on a tree stump.

He was in a bad mood. A very bad mood.

His friend Lena had come over, but she was playing with Brayden's sisters, Minnie and Millie. Lena was supposed to be Brayden's friend! He was going to show her his secret hiding place today—the one with the carrots.

HOME SWEET HOME

MOMMY MINNIE

MILLIE BRAYDEN

The girls wove flowers around
each other's ears.
"Silly," Brayden said to himself.

Then they pretended that their stuffed
animals were having a tea party.
"Even sillier," Brayden mumbled.

Next they sang a song.
"Come and join us!" called Lena,
but Brayden put his paws over his ears.

Finally, the three girls began to play hide-and-seek.

"Don't you want to play with us?" asked Lena.

"No!" growled Brayden. He spoiled their game by staring at them as they tried to hide so that each of the girls was found immediately.

If he couldn't enjoy himself, then why should his sisters?

SHED

"Let's play house on the garden chairs,"
suggested Millie.

"You can't!" said Brayden. "My train needs to go under the chairs."
"We thought of the chairs first!" Minnie shouted.
The siblings argued.

"Then we'll go for a walk instead," said Millie.
"As far away as possible!" said Brayden.
And that's just what the three girls did.

Brayden sat outside all alone.

Luckily, his friend Benny Badger happened to pass by.

Brayden loved playing with Benny.

"Where are your sisters?" asked Benny.

"Silly bunnies! We had an argument," said Brayden.

The two boys loaded the train cars with pebbles.

"Our trains are carrying gold," said Benny.

Brayden's eyes gleamed. "And robbers want to take the gold."

Benny looked up at the sky. It had turned very gray.

"There's a big storm on the way," he said. "Bertie Beaver warned me. He knows about these things."

"Minnie, Millie, and Lena scared stiff of thunder," Brayden said, looking anxiously at the clouds. "I have to go look for them."

"What?" said Benny. "You were just saying how silly they are."

Brayden's whiskers started to tremble. "Brothers and sisters have to look out for one another. They're all one family."

Brayden hurried away as fast as he could hop.

Benny stayed behind, shaking his head in disbelief.

Brayden ran across the field and met
Missy Mouse.

"Do you know where Minnie, Millie,
and Lena are?" he asked, panting.

"Down at the river," said Missy. "Why
do you want to know?"

But Brayden was already
on his way.
He had to find Minnie
and Millie!

There was nobody at the river except Fipsi Squirrel.
"I saw the three girls over in the big field," said Fipsi.
"What's the problem?"
But Brayden was already gone.

Minnie, Millie, and Lena weren't
in the big field, either.
And the clouds in the sky were
getting darker and darker.

"Maybe they're in the tree house," said Brayden hopefully.
He quickly climbed up the ladder.

While he was looking around, he heard voices outside.
It was Minnie, Millie, and Lena!
"Now let's go to the bridge to see the blue flowers," said
Millie enthusiastically.

Brayden climbed down the ladder and threw his paws around his sisters.

"What are you doing here?" asked Minnie angrily.

"Come home!" said Brayden urgently. "There's a big storm on the way. I came to get you because you're always so afraid of thunder and lightning."

"But so are you, Brayden," said Millie. "You get just as frightened as we do."

Brayden let out a sigh and nodded his head.
Minnie and Millie didn't look angry now.

In the distance they could hear a rumbling noise. "Let's
go home!"

"I'm not afraid," said Lena. "But we can't stay under
a tree when lightning comes."

The sky got darker and darker.

Together they all ran to the bunny house and closed the door nice and tight.

Suddenly, Minnie started to cry.

"Why are you crying?" asked Lena. "Everything's all right now."

"I'm crying because Brayden is so kind," sobbed Minnie. "Even though he was afraid, he came to find us."

Brayden went to his secret hiding place and brought back some carrots for everybody.

Just as the rain began to fall, Mommy Bunny came
hurrying home.

"I'm glad you're all here," she said.

"Brayden knew there was a storm on the way, so he
came and found us," said Millie.

"We saw something else, too," said Minnie.

"What's that?" asked Mommy Bunny.

"How nice brothers can be!" said Minnie.

Mommy Bunny said, "Nothing makes me smile more than seeing my bunnies so happy together."

Brayden returned to his hiding place and came back with the finest of all his carrots.

"This," he said, "is for Mommy."